ALSO BY SAM SWOPE

The Araboolies of Liberty Street
Pictures by Barry Root

The Krazees
Pictures by Eric Brace

Gotta Go! Gotta Go!
Pictures by Sue Riddle

JACK AND THE
SEVEN
DEADLY
GIANTS

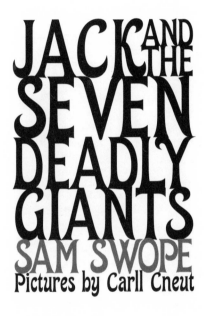

JACK AND THE SEVEN DEADLY GIANTS

SAM SWOPE

Pictures by Carll Cneut

Farrar, Straus and Giroux

New York

Text copyright © 2004 by Sam Swope
Pictures copyright © 2004 by Carll Cneut
All rights reserved
Distributed in Canada by Douglas & McIntyre Ltd.
Printed in the United States of America
Designed by Robbin Gourley
First edition, 2004
1   3   5   7   9   10   8   6   4   2

www.fsgkidsbooks.com

Library of Congress Cataloging-in-Publication Data
Swope, Sam.
     Jack and the seven deadly giants / Sam Swope; pictures by Carll Cneut.—
1st. ed.
        p.   cm.
     Summary: While hoping to find his mother, Jack encounters seven
deadly giants: The Giant Poet, The Terrible Glutton, Mrs. Roth, The
Wild Tickler, Avaritch, Orgulla the Great, and the Green Queen.
     ISBN 0-374-33670-9
     [1. Fairy tales.   2. Giants—Fiction.]   I. Cneut, Carll, ill.   II. Title.

PZ8.S9797Jac2004
[Fic]—dc22

                                                    2003054199

For Alessandro, Jim, and Nora,
and also for Jack,
who asked me once if I'd tell him a story

—S.S.

CONTENTS

PROLOGUE

Jack was just a bad boy, all the village said so. Everybody blamed it on he didn't have a mama, which he didn't, that was true.

Here's what happened.

Back when Jack was still a baby, he turned up one morning on the miller's doorstep, not a note to say where he was from, and he'd wailed and carried on so much the miller couldn't stand it, nor could anybody else, so Jack got left on doorstep after doorstep and he'd never had a proper home.

It went on like that and on, and then when Jack got older he was always in some trouble, didn't take to school, and either fell asleep in church or something worse, like what he did one Sunday way back when.

Jack hadn't meant to do a wrong. He tried his best to pay attention as the preacher waved his arms and carried on about the fire and the brimstone. But when the old man warned the congregation of the Seven Deadly Sins in words Jack didn't know, Jack thought he better learn them, so up he jumped and said, "Excuse me, sir. But I don't understand."

The church went hush.

No one ever dared before to interrupt the service, and the preacher wasn't pleased. He stormed down from his pulpit, grabbed Jack by the ear, said children should be seen, not heard, that Jack was bad, bad, bad, no boy was ever worse, and it wasn't any wonder his own mother didn't want him. Then he kicked Jack out the door.

Oh, Jack, poor Jack! No matter what he did, it never turned out good.

Not long after that, a stranger happened through the village. He said that on his travels he had heard a rumor there were giants in the land, and there were seven of them, awful creatures, deadly, too. Well, this was just such dreadful news that everyone got scared as scared could be. Women fainted. Men did, too.

Everybody ran to see the preacher, begged him please to save them. They all cried, "What can we do?"

But seven deadly sins were one thing, seven deadly real-live giants something else, and that old preacher didn't have a clue. He stammered, stuttered, hemmed and hawed, and then he got the thought to blame the whole calamity on Jack, said Jack must be a curse, that bad attracts bad, and thanks to Jack those seven deadly giants sure would come and be the ruination of them all.

Hearing that made Jack feel sorry in his heart for being bad. He didn't want to bring the village harm, and seeing it was all his fault, Jack figured that the only thing to do was go away so they'd be safe. No one tried to stop him, they were glad to see him go: Good riddance and goodbye!

And so it was, with just an apple in his pocket, Jack wandered off along the dusty road, no notion where he might be headed, and the world was all before him, big and wide. He walked and walked, went on, went on, till by and by he met a funny little man.

"Hello," said Jack.

"Hello," said the funny little man. "You got a bit of food to spare? My stomach's growlin' somethin' awful."

"Sure I do. It's lunchtime anyhow. Let's eat."

They sat together by the roadside and Jack divvied up the apple, half and half. After they had eaten, the funny little man said he was much obliged and handed Jack a bean, a bean he said was magic, good for just a single wish.

Jack was pleased. One wish was all he needed, since there wasn't but a single wish in all the world he'd ever had. He closed his fingers round the bean and said, "I want my mother."

But when he opened up his eyes in hopes to see his mom, Jack got an awful shock to see a cow instead. She was white and brown with horns and great big eyes that stared at Jack all warm and quiet.

"Moo," said the cow.

"The wish don't work," said Jack. "Must be your bean is broke."

But no one answered. The funny little man had up and gone. Jack scratched his head. The cow, meanwhile, was on her way and plodding down the road. She stopped to look around at Jack as if to ask what was he waiting for.

"She thinks she's mine," thought Jack,

and he supposed she was, since he had wished her, in a way.

"Wait up!" called Jack, and ran to get the cow. She waited patient as he struggled, climbing on her back, but somehow Jack got all his arms and legs so mixed up and confused he wound up facing backward. Jack wondered for a moment if he ought to change, then decided he'd stay put, and always ever after rode like that, the wrong way round, so he could look at all the places he had been and be surprised by anyplace he got.

THE GIANT POET

Seemed to Jack that nothing could be nicer, riding backward on a cow. He stretched out flat and made himself a pillow with his hands. What a day! The sun was warm, the sky was blue, and Jack thought he'd be happy just to keep that up forever, never doing anything but counting clouds.

Lost in lazy dreaming, Jack didn't keep a sharp eye out, which anyone should do when on an unfamiliar road, and that was why Jack failed to see the giant up ahead who loafed beneath a willow tree and chewed a piece of grass.

The giant, though, spied Jack. And when he saw that Jack was heading toward him down the road, that giant went as still as any cat. He held his breath and waited till the cow passed by, then snatched Jack off her back.

"Hey! Put me down!"

"Don't be scared," the giant said, and petted Jack like he was just a kitten. "What's your name, boy?"

The giant was as skinny as a stick and had a gentle face. Jack figured that he wasn't in much danger and calmed down. "Jack," he said. "My name is Jack."

The giant's face lit up all pleased. "Ah, Jack! Now there's a fine poetic name! There are so many Jacks in poetry: Jack Sprat, Jack and Jill, Jack Be Nimble . . ."

"Little Jack Horner," added Jack.

"True, true!" the giant said. "And I, dear Jack, am Sloth, the Giant Poet."

"Heck," said Jack. "I never met a real live poet before."

"Would you like to hear one of my poems?"

"I guess I would."

Sloth heaved a giant sigh. "Oh, so would I, Jack! So would I! But I am sorry to report that I have yet to write a single one. I tell you, Jack, it's such a torture being me! Sometimes I get the most wonderful idea for a poem, but when it comes to writing out the words, well, it all begins to seem like such a bother that I get discouraged. So I end up doing nothing and it isn't long before my inspiration is forgotten and the poem lost."

"That's a shame," Jack said.

"More than a shame. It's tragic!"

The silly giant looked so down-and-out

that Jack felt kind of sorry for him. "Maybe I could help," he said.

"Help? How?"

"You could say your poem out and I could write it down."

"What a brilliant idea! You'll be my scribe!"

Sloth pulled out the satchel he had tucked behind the tree and dug inside it for supplies. When he found his pencil, he was pleased to see its point was just as sharp as when he'd packed it all those years before. Then he took his journal out, opened it up flat, and set Jack on the huge first page.

The giant's pencil was a good head taller than was Jack, but Jack discovered if he leaned it up against his shoulder he could drag it 'cross the page and write. He asked the giant, "What's the title?"

Sloth thought that over for a while, then said, "I will call my poem *Magnum Opus.*"

"What's that?"

"It's Latin, Jack, and means this poem will be my greatest work."

"That's a good idea," said Jack. "How's *Magnum Opus* spelled?"

The giant got annoyed and said, "What do I look like, a dictionary? Stop ruining my concentration, boy, and get to work."

Jack spelled the title out as best he could but found it wasn't easy writing words in giant letters. Each straight line took several steps, and making sure the *O* in *Opus* wound up nice and round required lots of concentration. But by and by Jack finished up, and then the giant said, "Now, under that write: *by Sloth, the Giant Poet.*"

So Jack wrote that down, too, and asked the giant what came next.

"What comes next, dear Jack, is a little *quelque chose*."

"What's that?"

"It's French, my boy, and in this particular instance, *quelque chose* means 'snack.'"

Sloth took out bread and cheese and wine and offered several giant crumbs to Jack. As they ate, the giant said, "Many poets believe they have to starve themselves, dear Jack, but that is foolish thinking. Remember this, my boy: the imagination needs nourishment just as much as the body."

After they had polished off the *quelque chose*, Jack took the pencil up to write some more, but then the giant said they'd worked

enough and he was finished for the day.
Sloth yawned, he stretched, he said, "Poems
can't be forced, dear Jack, for poems are
like flowers. They grow at their own pace
and only blossom when they're ready. Be-
sides, my friend, a poet needs his sleep. For
when a poet sleeps, he dreams, and in his
dreams the muse may come and offer inspiration."

What happened next took Jack all un-
awares. The giant picked him up and stuck
Jack underneath the giant's hat!

"Hey! What are you doing? Let me go!"

"I'm afraid I can't do that, Jack. I need
you."

"I'm not your slave!"

"Ah, but you are, Jack! You are! Yet do

not look so sad. Take heart! I, too, am a slave—a slave to poetry. You must embrace your fate, my boy, as I have embraced mine. Destiny has chosen us! Be grateful!"

With that, the giant curled up, shut his lazy eyes, and fell asleep.

So there Jack was, a prisoner. As Sloth snored, Jack puzzled for a while what he might do, then had to puzzle more, but finally he got a plan and rapped his knuckles on the giant's head.

"Wake up! Hey, Sloth! Wake up! Your muse was here!"

The giant gave a start. "What's that? My muse was here? How exciting! What did she say?"

"She inspired you so much you said a

poem in your sleep, and I had better get the words down quick or I'll forget!"

"Yes, yes, you're right, a poet has to strike while the iron is hot! We must to work at once!"

Sloth set Jack back on the journal, and Jack got to writing straightaway. All the while the giant told him hurry, hurry, hurry, and when at last Jack put the pencil down, Sloth snatched the journal, cleared his throat, and in his most poetic voice he read aloud his poem . . .

MAGNUM OPUS
by Sloth, the Giant Poet

Once there was a poet.
He was very, very tall,
And so very, very lazy
That he never wrote at all.

19

The giant wrinkled up his face, all disappointed. "It's rather short for a *magnum opus*, don't you think?"

"Not at all," said Jack. "I think it's first-rate. I mean, not every poem in the world is long. You got 'Humpty Dumpty,' 'Hickory, Dickory, Dock!' . . ."

"True enough, Jack. True enough! Not to mention 'Hey Diddle Diddle!' and 'Mary, Mary, Quite Contrary' . . . classics all! Perhaps I've been too hasty in my judgment. Let me read my *Magnum Opus* once again."

"Good idea," said Jack.

Sloth read his poem out again and then again. Each time, he liked it better and in the end decided Jack was right: his *Magnum Opus* was a work of genius. Sloth was so pleased he thought he'd go to sleep and write

20

another one, but when he looked around for Jack he saw his scribe was on his cow and clear off down the valley, hurrying away.

It would have been an easy thing for Sloth to run and catch the boy, but even just the thought of all that effort wore the giant out. And anyway, what was the point? Sloth told himself, "One masterpiece is more than most poets manage and all the world can reasonably expect of any poet. No, I've done my part. I've earned the right to rest upon my laurels."

And with that, the giant leaned against the willow tree and rested on his laurels for the rest of his days.

THE TERRIBLE
GLUTTON

Going on, going on, and Jack was getting hungry. He perked up happy when the cow found them a tree with pears all tasty ripe. The cow was hungry, too. She raised her head to eat but couldn't reach the fruit, so Jack climbed up the tree and tossed some down.

Chomp, chomp.

Jack watched her large jaws work the pears. Even if she wasn't much for talk, Jack guessed the cow was just about the best friend any boy had ever had. Look at all she did for him! She carried him around all day, lay beside him warm at night, and in the morning gave him milk to drink. She did all this, plus never once told Jack that he was bad. No one in the village ever treated him as good, so it wasn't any wonder Jack had come to love her best of all.

The cow looked up at Jack, wanting him to throw another pear.

Chomp, chomp.

After she'd had her fill, the cow went to a nearby stream and drank while Jack stayed in the tree and ate.

Chomp, chomp.

Those pears were awful good, the sweetest Jack had ever tasted, and he couldn't get enough.

Chomp, chomp.

Jack stuffed his face till he got sick and burped, the smell of which was carried downwind to a giant, which was not a lucky chance.

Sniff! Sniff!

This was the Terrible Glutton, and he was just a monstrous beast that only lived to eat and eat and eat. Everywhere he went, the Glutton gobbled anything he came across and never even stopped to cook it. He swallowed birds and bears and kitty cats down live. He ate up all the farmers' crops and all the soil to boot. Whatever he could grab, the Glutton didn't care—he'd even rip a tree from out the ground and swallow it down whole!

SLOBBER SLOBBER SNORT GRUNT GRUNT!

The Glutton ate so much that everything on him was fat, fat, fat. His nose was fat, his ears were fat, his eyes were fat, and every single hair on him was fat, fat, fat! He had so many chins he couldn't see his shoulders! His belly was so fat it covered up his legs like he had on a skirt! You never saw a more disgusting and revolting creature than that Glutton in your whole entire life!

Sniff! Sniff!

The Glutton smelled Jack's burp and knew at once it was a boy's, and that gave him a smile. His favorite food! Yum-yum!

Poor Jack! He never knew what hit him. Never had a chance. That giant bore down fast and plucked Jack from the tree and dangled him above his mouth like Jack was just a grape.

SLOBBER SLOBBER SNORT GRUNT GRUNT!

"Hey! What are you doing?" cried Jack.

"I'm going to eat you," said the Glutton.

"You can't do that!"

"I'm the Terrible Glutton. I can do anything I want."

"That's no fair! You have to give me a chance to save myself!"

The Glutton paused to think on that, and then decided he could have a bit of fun before he ate the boy.

"I'll tell you what," the giant said. "If you come up with something I can't eat, I set you free. If you fail, I eat you up. You get three chances. Deal?"

"Deal," said Jack, and hid a smirk that showed he thought that this would be a cinch.

The giant smirked as well. He knew Jack

couldn't win. There was nothing that the Glutton couldn't eat. Nothing!

Jack got started right away. He mixed up moss and mold and mildew with a bunch of slimy snails and leeches and a mess of green gunk from a pond as well as other things too gross to mention, things that stank so bad Jack had to hold his nose.

P.U.!

Jack told the giant, "No one with a brain would eat this."

"Too bad for you, 'cause I don't have a brain," the Glutton said, and stuck his face inside the muck and sucked up every bit of it. "Not bad," he said, and licked his lips. "What's next?"

Oh, no!

This time Jack got every poison thing that he could find—deadly snakes, spiders, mushrooms, and berries—and chopped them up together for a salad, saying, "This here is a dish to die for."

"We'll see about that," the Glutton said, and shoved it in his big fat mouth and bolted it right down. Jack watched the giant's face go gray and squinch up in such awful pain that Jack was sure he was about to drop down dead.

Hooray!

But then, instead, the giant let loose with a most gigantic fart, a fart so huge that it was like the thunder, blew a crater in the ground, and knocked Jack off his feet.

BOOM!

After all the air was clear, the Glutton sat there smiling, rubbed his tummy, asked Jack were there maybe seconds.

Oh, no, again!

Two chances down and only one to go! Jack's stomach was tied up in knots! His goose was cooked for sure! He stalled as best he could to give himself some time to think, and all the while the Glutton drooled, because Jack looked so good to eat.

Finally the giant couldn't wait another second, so he said, "Time's up! I win!" and went to stuff Jack in his mouth.

"Wait!" cried Jack. "I know a thing that you can't eat!"

"Fat chance!"

"Yourself!" said Jack. "You cannot eat yourself!"

"Who says I can't?" said the Terrible Glutton. "And after I'm done eating me, I'm eating you!"

What happened next was not a pretty sight. The giant started with his toes. They were tastier than he expected, like sausages but crunchy. "Yum-yum," he said. Next he tucked into his legs and they were good, good, good, way juicier than drumsticks. "I should have eaten me years ago!" the Glutton cried, and gorged himself upon his belly, which was so delicious that the Glutton thought he'd died and gone to heaven.

SLOBBER SLOBBER SNORT GRUNT GRUNT!

In no time flat the only part left to be eaten was the giant's head, but how to get it in his mouth confused the Glutton and he stopped to chew the problem over.

"Hmmm," the giant said.

"You have to eat yourself up every bit or else I win!" cried Jack.

"I will! I will! Just wait and see!" And that determined Glutton got to grunting and to straining. He worked his jaws and forced his mouth to open wider and wider and then wider still. As his upper lip inched over the top of his head and his lower lip went underneath, he thought, "I've got me now!"

There comes a time in every swallow when the swallow pauses for a second as the muscles in the mouth stop working and the muscles in the throat take over. Once a swallow's got that far, though, there is no turning back, no way to stop it. And at just that very moment, when it was too late, the Glutton figured out what was about to happen. "But if I eat me—" he said, then never made another sound, except the final gulp that showed he'd swallowed his own head inside out and disappeared.

Poof!

MRS. ROTH

When the sun came up, the dark sky turned a rosy pink. It was sure to be a pretty day, but giant Mrs. Roth was miffed. She lay in bed and snarled up at the sun, "Who asked you to rise? And on my birthday, too!" She stuck her head under her pillow. She tossed and turned and flipped and flopped. She got her knickers in a twist. *"Errrrgggh,"* she growled.

Then Mrs. Roth got out the wrong side of the bed, threw on a robe, and stuck her head out the window. "Frikken frik frak sun!" she shouted. The sun ignored her, though, which got the giant's dander up. In a snit, she scowled, and as she yanked her head in-side, she thwacked it on the window.

"Ouch!"

Mrs. Roth was so ticked off, she didn't see her dog beneath her feet and stepped right on his tail. *"Yowlll!"*

"Frikken frik frak dog!" cried Mrs. Roth. She snatched the mutt and tossed him out the window, where he landed on the cat, who shrieked and leapt in through the window, where she landed on the giant's butt and dug her claws in tight.

"Ouch!"

That got the giant seeing red. She tried to grab the cat but couldn't reach, so she took out her broom and swung it backward over the top of her head, and when the cat jumped clear—WHOMP!—the giant whacked her own rear end.

"Frikken frik frak cat!" cried Mrs. Roth. Oooooh, was she mad! She was madder than a wet hen! She chased the cat all over everywhere! She smacked her broom at anything that wound up in the way! She raised all kinds of Cain! Lamps crashed! Chairs smashed! Plates shattered! The giant got so worked up that she flipped her lid, which drove her up the wall, which sent her through the roof, which hurt her giant head.

Mrs. Roth looked at the sky. There sat the stupid sun, smug as ever, shining down all bright and cheery. This was the limit! She'd had it up to here!

"*Errrrgggh!*"

Mrs. Roth was foaming at the mouth. She raced down to her garden, grabbed the hose, and turned the spigot on full blast to douse the sun and drown it all to bits. The sun kept right on shining, though, which really got the giant's goad. She hurled some rocks up at the sun, but one went wrong and hit a hornets' nest and got those hornets so het up they took off after Mrs. Roth and chased her over fields and sent her round the bend— "Ootch! Ouch!"—till finally the only way she could escape was by jumping in the pond.

Splash!

What a lousy, awful birthday Mrs. Roth was having!

The giant kept her head under the water till the coast was clear—*glug, glug*—and when

she peeked up out at last, who did she spy but
Jack. He was only just a ways away atop a
hill, and she could see that he was hopping
mad. He waved his arms all angry at his cow,
who wouldn't budge, just stared at him and
chewed her cud.

Jack had good reason to be all upset.
He'd heard a fearful ruckus not far back,
some awful shouting, dishes breaking, and
he worried that giants were about. He
shouted, "Move! Would you get moving?"
but the cow, she only stood there, stubborn
as a rock.

Mrs. Roth crept out from the pond and
crouched behind a bush. *"Oooooeeee!"* she
thought. "This is my lucky day!" It wasn't
very often that she spotted any boys. She'd
had one as a pet when she was just a child

and thought it would be fine if on her birth-day she could snag herself another. The giant only wished she'd brought along her net—it's not an easy thing to catch a boy bare-handed!

Up the hill, Jack went back behind the cow and set his shoulder to her haunch. He pushed and pushed, but all she did was turn her head and look at him in wonder what he was about. Jack got hot under the collar. He stomped up front, grabbed her rope, and pulled with all his might—"Move, you stupid cow!"—but then the cow jerked back, which yanked the rope, which broke Jack's grip, which sent him down the hill head over heels and right into the waiting hands of Mrs. Roth.

"Happy birthday to me!" she cried.

The giant held Jack in her fist so only just

his head was sticking out. She made some kissing noises at him, told him he was cute, then stuffed him in her bathrobe pocket, brought him home, and locked him in a birdcage.

Mrs. Roth gave Jack a dish of milk and went and got her birthday cake. "Chocolate!" she told him. "Want some?" The giant put some icing on her finger, stuck it through the bars, and when Jack bit it—"Ouch!"—old Mrs. Roth went bonkers. She stomped her feet and carried on so bad, Jack worried she would have a cow. To calm her down, he started singing "Happy Birthday."

Ooh! Ah! Why, giant Mrs. Roth could not believe her ears! She'd never in her life heard anything so pretty and so sweet, and just like that she cooled right off, her anger melted clean away. She sat down in her comfy chair and listened with an almost-smile across her face.

When the song was done, the giant's face went dark and stormy. "More!" she cried, and pounded with her fists.

Jack could see he had no choice and so he sang another song, but then she wanted still another and another and another. It went on like that and on till Jack had sung her every song he knew and some he didn't, but the giant always cried out, "More! More! More!" and when the sun began to set Jack got the thought to sing a lullaby.

"Louder!" ordered Mrs. Roth.

"A lullaby you can't sing loud," said Jack. "Put me by your ear and you'll hear fine."

Mrs. Roth took Jack from out the cage

and set him on her shoulder. He sat beside her ear and sang as soft and sweet as he could sing, and by and by the giant's eyes got heavy and her head began to nod and finally she fell asleep and started breathing deep and slow. Jack kept singing, nervous she might wake, and as he sang he crept out on her chest, then worked his way down to her lap and tiptoed 'cross her thigh. From there he grabbed hold of her bathrobe belt and shinnied to the carpet.

He looked up at the giant. She was still sleeping sound, so Jack guessed it was safe to let his singing taper off, and by the time he reached the door he slipped away in silence.

Outside, night was coming fast. Jack was overjoyed to see his cow waiting in the shadows. He cried and hugged her neck and told her he was sorry he had yelled and called her stupid, said that it was all his fault and that he'd always been a bad boy. He begged her to forgive him, but she didn't say a thing, so Jack just climbed up on her back and off they disappeared into the night.

Several hours later, Mrs. Roth woke up. When she saw her boy had flown the coop, she started bawling, raced outside. She beat her chest and cried, "Please, boy, please come back! I promise to be nice and won't be angry anymore! Oh, please! I love you, boy!"

But Jack, he didn't answer, and that sure got the giant riled. She hollered, "Frikken frik frak boy! Just you wait till I find you!" She stormed into the country, determined she would catch the boy and drag him back, but it was dark and hard to see. She stepped into a cow pie. "Yech!" She shook her fist up at the sky and hollered, "Frikken frik frak sun! Where are you when I need you?"

The giant was so blind with rage she couldn't find Jack anywhere, and that just burned her up. *"Errrrgggh!"* cried Mrs. Roth. She ranted, raved, she got so steamed she started fuming and her blood began to boil! She blew a gasket! She was spitting nails! Oh, no! She flipped her wig! She popped her cork! Look out! That giant, she was ready to explode! Duck and cover! Mrs. Roth just blew her stack!

KABOOM!

THE WILD TICKLER

Looking left, looking right, looking back, looking front, and nothing anywhere but sand, sand, sand. Not a cloud was in the sky and it was oven hot. Jack's mouth was dry as dust and he was drenched in sweat. He tied his shirt around his head to make a turban. The cow went on.

The day got hotter, so hot Jack got dizzy. The desert started looking quivery, like the world was underwater, and that's when Jack saw a mirage that seemed so true he thought it really was the farmer's daughter from back home. She'd been older than Jack by seven years at least, cherry-lipped and freckle-faced and pretty as a picture. But the preacher called her wicked, said she only ever wanted to be kissing, kissing, kissing, and when once the farmer's daughter winked at Jack in church, he went all butterflies and blushed.

And now Jack saw, or thought he saw, her waving at him 'cross the desert—throwing kisses!—and his heart, it got to racing pitter-pat. He cried, "Hey, there. Hi! It's me, Jack!" She didn't answer, though, and then Jack watched in misery to see the farmer's daughter strangely fade away and vanish, nothing left but air. "No!" cried Jack. "Come back!" But she was gone, and that was that.

On they went.

The sun beat down, beat down, and Jack became so overheated and exhausted that he fainted. When he came to, he found himself

on an oasis underneath a lemon tree where it
was cool. The cow was slurping water from a
spring. Jack lay down beside her and stuck
his head into the water.

Ahhhhh!

After both were feeling more themselves,
the cow lay down to rest and Jack picked up
some lemons. He stuffed them in his pockets,
thinking later on he'd make some lemonade.

Meanwhile, up behind some rocks, a giant hid and watched Jack's every move.

Tickle-wickle! Tickle-wickle!

Oh, Jack, poor Jack! He was a goner and
he didn't even know it. He'd been spotted by
the Wild Tickler, a vicious thing with two gigantic heads. One head was called Her, the
other Him. Her had bushy bright-red hair,

but Him was bald and had a bushy bright-red beard. Both sets of eyes, both Her's and Him's, were dark and overeager.

Tickle-wickle! Tickle-wickle!

The cruel Tickler spent its days out on the prowl to find something to tickle. Anything that breathed would do—a bird, a snake, a turtle. The Tickler moved so fast that nothing could escape it, and all creatures lived in terror of the beast 'cause once that giant had you in its clutches it would tickle you to death.

Tickle-wickle! Tickle-wickle!

The Tickler had an instinct, knew just where to find a body's tickle spots. On dogs, the perfect spot was up behind a leg. On rabbits, at the bottom inside of an ear. For squirrels, the Tickler tickled underneath the chin, and bugs went wild when that old giant got to working on their feelers.

Run, Jack! Run!

Tickle-wickle! Tickle-wickle!

Him saw Jack first and whispered in Her's ear, "Oooooh, lookee off what's come to us down over there!"

Her gave a gasp. "Oh, my! Could it be boy?"

"Aye, sure it is."

The giant was so tickled pink it gave a prayer of thanks. Nothing on Earth was better for a tickle than a boy! Nothing squealed and squirmed and cried for mercy near so good!

"Get 'im quick!"

The Tickler tore off down the rocks, its arms all waving crazy as it shrieked its battle cry. In a blink it held Jack tight.

"Keep your mitts off me!" shouted Jack. He kicked and bit as best he could, but that coldhearted giant didn't pay him any mind, just held him up and looked him over good for where his tickle spot would be.

"It's years since we did tickle boy," said Him.

"Our last one laughed so hard it split its sides!"

"It bust its gut! Oh, what a sight were that! Boy insides were spillin' out all over! Yes, yes! I did a brilliant tickle then."

Her said, "No matter what, still fair is fair. You did the last, so this boy here be mine. You take the cow."

"Cow's no fun! You have to share. I saw boy first."

"All right, you can, but not till after me."

Her got herself warmed up. She cracked her knuckles, flexed her tickle fingers good, then started making slow, slow circles with them down toward Jack.

Tickle-wickle! Tickle-wickle!

Jack cried, "No!" and watched in horror. Closer came those fingers, closer still. He tightened every muscle, closed his eyes. He cried out, "Help me! Help!" but no one heard, it wasn't any use.

Tickle-wickle! Tickle-wickle!

Just before Her's fingers hit, Jack got a flash about what he should do. He grabbed a lemon from his pocket, popped it in his mouth, and bit down hard to fill his mouth with juice so sour that it shocked the tickle clean away. He didn't laugh a bit. He didn't even chuckle.

"What's wrong?" said Her. "Boy's giggler must be broke."

"Stuff and nonsense," said Him. "You just got old and lost your touch. Now quick, get out the way and let me show you how it's proper done."

Him got to work and tried his best, but it was just the same. Jack didn't crack a smile. Him looked disgusted, said, "It be defective boy we got us here."

"Let's do the cow!"

The Tickler let Jack go and snagged the cow. It flipped her over belly up. Poor thing, you never saw a more pathetic sight, her legs all kicking wild as she was bellowing for mercy.

Jack couldn't stand to see her suffer and he shouted out, "Just let her be and I'll show you the secret trick to tickle me!"

"What's that?" the Tickler said, and let go of the cow to give its full attention back to Jack. "Quick, teach us! Teach!"

"All we need is feathers," said Jack.

"Feathers we can do!" the giant said.

While the giant rummaged round for feathers in whatever birds' nests it could find, Jack took off his shoes and socks and sat down with his back against the tree and both his feet stuck out.

Soon enough, some feathers had been found and everything was ready. Jack said, "See those spaces in between my toes?"

"Yes, yes! We see!"

"When I say 'go,' put the feathers in there and then twirl 'em slow for five times to the right, then left for eight, then do it all again except go fast the other way but in reverse."

The Tickler looked confused.

"Now, here's the most important part," said Jack. "You have to say the magic words. Listen good and repeat after me: cootchee."

Him and Her answered as one: "Cootchee!"

"Again."

"Cootchee!"

"Now say 'coo.' "

"Coo!"

"Okay, put them all together: cootchee cootchee coo."

"Cootchee cootchee coo!"

"Again: cootchee cootchee coo."

"Cootchee cootchee coo! Cootchee cootchee coo!"

"Perfect!" said Jack. "I think you're ready."

Her slobbered. Him slavered.

Jack said, "On your mark . . . get set . . ." But then before Jack could say "Go!" the Tickler pounced, so much excited it forgot the rules and tickled Jack all anyhow. But Jack, he didn't mind one bit. With his trusty lemon in his mouth, he just sat there, peaceful as a pickle.

The Tickler got annoyed. "Your tickle do not work," it said.

"That's because you didn't follow my directions," Jack said. "I guess I have to demonstrate."

"Ooh, good idea! So let's, and hurry, too!"

They traded places. Jack stuck the feathers in between the giant's toes, which made the Tickler lurch and give a squeal. But when Jack got to saying "Cootchee cootchee coo!" and turned those feathers round, the Tickler went wild.

"Ooh! Stop! Eeeh! Hee! Stop! Skeech! Stop!"

"It's all in the wrist," Jack explained.

"Oh! Stop! Ah! Hoo! Eeeh! Stop! Haw! Skeech!"

By and by Jack figured he had done enough and stopped. The Tickler was so worn out and exhausted it just sat there, heaving happy. "Oh, that were the bestest tickle ever. More! Please, more!"

"Now practice on each other," Jack suggested.

"Oh yes! Let's tickle us! Quick, quick!"

And so they did.

"Hee! Skeech! Haw! Ooh!"

It's hard to say which head laughed

harder, Her's or Him's. Him cried out for Her to stop, and Her begged Him for mercy, but both were howling out so loud that neither heard the other, and it wasn't long before the Tickler laughed so hard it laughed its heads right off and never laughed again.

Goodbye!

AVARITCH

"Ghosts could live in swampy woods like these," thought Jack, "or maybe goblins. Trolls." There was a dank and moldy smell, and everything was shadowy and dark from all the twisted, tangled branches overhead. From time to time, a wind blew through the trees and made them moan.

When night came on, the cow lay down and Jack stayed close beside her till he heard a voice come through the forest. It was counting.

"Three million one . . . three million two . . . three million three . . ."

Jack crept off to see. Not far away he

found a cave, and from it came a golden glowing light. Jack peeked in and gave a gasp. The cave was bigger than the belly of a whale and all full up with piles on piles of gold. In the middle of that mess of loot sat Avaritch, a giant with a pointy onion face and squinty eyes made weak from counting out his money.

"Three million four . . . three million five . . ."

Avaritch was filthy rich but he was born dirt poor. Getting wealthy sure had not been easy, though. Avaritch had got his start by selling his own mother. With that money he'd then lied and cheated and cheated and lied till finally he'd built the fortune he was counting now.

The giant licked the drool from off his lips and numbered up his lucre.

"Three million six . . . three million seven . . . three million eight . . ."

First thing every morning, Avaritch would see his gold, and there was such an awful lot of it, just piles and pretty piles, that it would put a smile across his greedy face, and he would start the morning out by rolling in it, happy as a dog in dirt. "Mine, mine, all mine!" he'd cry.

Then he'd get to wondering exactly how much gold he really had, and so he'd start to count it out.

"Three million nine . . . three million ten . . ."

The only problem was, the more gold that the giant counted, the less was left to count. As Avaritch would see his counting pile grow smaller, he'd get increasing worried, bite his nails and wring his hands. And when he'd counted every scrap of gold he had, he'd beat his chest and cry out he was broke and ruined, headed for the poorhouse!

"More gold, I need more gold! More gold!" he'd whimper till he cried himself to sleep.

Come the morning, Avaritch would rub the sleep from out his eyes and look about him. When he saw that, yes, he really did have lots of gold, just gobs and gorgeous gobs, more gold than ninety hundred kings could spend in ninety hundred lifetimes, oh how his greedy little heart would sing! And then he'd start to count it out again.

"One . . . two . . . three . . ."

Jack stood there at the entrance to the cave, all openmouthed. He couldn't pry his eyes from off that gold, and started thinking how he wanted to be rich. Not overrich, he wasn't greedy. Only just a little gold would do. A single bag is all he'd need. Or two, one for his cow. Or maybe three. No, four. Or why not five?

Jack hatched a scheme. He used his shirt to make a sack, filled it up with rocks, then tied the sleeves up tight. He acted like he had been dragging it for days and called out loud to make the giant hear, "Boy, this gold is heavy!"

Avaritch was startled, stopped his counting, cocked his head to hear. Had somebody said "gold"? The giant scurried out the cave to see. His eyes weren't good, he had to squint into the night. He shouted, "Who goes there?"

"It's only me, a boy named Jack."

"Gold? Did you say 'gold'?"

"Yes, sir. I said this bag of gold is heavy!"

"Where'd a boy like you get gold?"

"I got lucky! I done found the Road to Riches!"

Avaritch gasped. More famous than the rainbow's pot of gold, the Road to Riches was a legend in those parts, a roadway made of gold that just went on forever, never any end. Sometimes at night the giant dreamed that he had found the Road to Riches, but then always just before he reached it, he'd wake up, the dream would stop, and all his happiness would vanish.

Jack said, "Soon as I get home, I'm headin' straight back there again and then again till I got gold enough to set me up for life."

The giant's mind worked fast, calculating out his profit and his loss, his risk and his gain. He said to Jack, "If you show me the Road to Riches, boy, I'll give you twenty bags of gold and save you the trouble of making all those trips."

Jack acted like he had to think that over. He wrinkled up his face, he tugged his ear, so then the giant offered thirty bags, but Jack said, "Gee, sir, I don't rightly know . . ."

The giant clenched his fists, he bit his lip. Whatever was the price, he had to find that road! "I'll give you fifty bags, is that enough?"

"Hmmm."

"All right, a hundred, then, you little swindler!"

"It's a deal," said Jack, and tried his best to hide his glee. He'd really pulled a fast one!

Woo-hoo! A hundred bags of gold! Oh, Jack was rich, rich, rich!

The giant growled, "Wait here," and went inside the cave. It was a painful thing for Avaritch to part with gold, but he took comfort from the thought that once he'd found the Road to Riches, he'd have wealth beyond his wildest dreams.

Jack waited happy, thinking of the mansion he would buy, and in a while the giant came from out the cave, pushing an enormous cart filled up with just a hundred bags exactly. "Here's your gold," he said to Jack.

"Thank you kindly," Jack replied, and tossed his sack among the others. "Now let me draw you out a map. The Road to Riches isn't far. If you get started soon, then I expect that you'll be there by the morning."

AVARITCH

What happened next showed Jack what greed can do. The giant's face went hard and sharp as any knife. He clutched his bony hand around Jack's throat and squeezed it tight till Jack began to sputter and choke and gasp for air. The giant said, "I know your game. You'll make a phony map and send me off the wrong way round so you can keep the Road to Riches for yourself! Well, no one makes a fool of Avaritch! You don't get a single piece of gold till you have brought me to the Road to Riches, and you better hadn't cheat me, boy, or you'll be sorry. Understand?"

Oh, Jack! Things hadn't gone the way he planned, and now he didn't know what he could do except pretend he knew the way. He climbed up on the cow and off they went, cart and all, into the woods. Every now and then Jack said, "Go right here" or "Here it's to the left," but it was plain he couldn't keep this fooling up forever.

They traveled far. And sure enough, as night wore on, the giant got complaining that the trip was taking much too long.

"We're getting there," lied Jack. He tried and tried but couldn't find a plan to save himself, so it was lucky when a plan found him. A full moon rose and sat above the far horizon like a giant golden eye, and when the ground gave way to sand and Jack began to smell the sea, he cried out, "It's not far now, just up ahead!"

"Hurry!" cried the giant.

Jack brought the giant up atop a dune that overlooked a sea all calm and black except for where the moonlight shimmered on its surface like a sparkly pathway leading off to heaven. The giant squinted, saw, and fell down on his knees to thank his lucky stars. He'd found it! Yes! The Road to Riches! Without a word he hurried down, his arms outstretched, a greedy silhouette that danced out on that shining roadway and then quickly vanished, swallowed by the sea.

Jack didn't know if Avaritch could swim and didn't wait to see. But when he turned to get his gold, Jack found that all those hundred bags were full of just potatoes.

Avaritch had tricked him!

ORGULLA THE GREAT

Perhaps, thought Jack, there had been other boys who'd battled giants, but he bet none had bested near so many. Jack was preening, he felt proud, there wasn't anything in all the world he couldn't do. And when they came upon a huge and jagged mountain range, Jack wasn't bothered, not a bit. "Heck," he said. "I'll climb those easy! Giddyap!"

Then Jack sat tight and let his cow begin the journey up.

And up.

And up.

The higher they went, the colder it got.

There were rocks and snow and stubby, scraggy trees. As they came near the mountain's peak, Jack figured that the worst was over, but from the top he saw they'd only just begun.

For miles ahead were only mountains, nothing but mountains, oceans of mountains, and mountains forever.

The cow just kept her head down, eyes fixed on the path. One step at a time, that's the way you conquer mountains. For days they traveled, up one peak, then down its other side, then up another, down and up and up and down. In all that time they didn't meet another soul, their only company the wind.

Somewhere in the middle of that range, a single peak rose higher than the rest. This was the home of Orgulla the Great. She stood up on her mountain, proud to be the greatest, most gigantic giant of them all. Even the gods adored her! Why else would they have put her on the highest peak if not so she'd be closer to them up in heaven? And who could blame the gods for that? Who wouldn't want so wonderful a giant near? No one had a prettier eye than Orgulla the Great, or one so nicely centered on her forehead! No one had a finer nose, or one so long it grew down to her toes!

Orgulla shouted to the mountains, "Hail, all hail Orgulla the Great!" and when the echoes echoed back, they bounced off other mountains, making other echoes, and those echoes made still other echoes till a thousand echoes cried out, "Hail, all hail Orgulla the Great . . . the Great . . . the Great!" but what Orgulla thought she heard instead was hosts of giants singing out her praises.

Pity Orgulla, Orgulla the Great! It isn't easy being perfect, not a bit. Beauty always pays a price! It's lonely at the top! But when Orgulla got to feeling sorry for herself, she'd say, "Orgulla, someone has to be the best, and if the gods have chosen you, then you must play your part."

At any rate, Orgulla knew she'd be rewarded. The gods would not forget. She was certain one day they'd make her a star, if not a whole entire constellation.

"Hail, all hail Orgulla the Great . . . the Great . . . the Great!"

Orgulla heard a noise. Footsteps! She had a visitor! Her very first! Orgulla rushed to see who it might be. "Oh, my!" Orgulla gasped, unable to believe her eye. She wondered was she dreaming, pinched herself, and looked again. But sure enough, she had seen right: a god was coming up to pay her his respects! It had to be a god, for nothing else could be so huge that next to him Orgulla the Great was just as small as any bug.

The only strange thing that Orgulla couldn't understand was why the god was sitting backward on a cow . . .

Proud Orgulla, foolish thing! Because she'd spent her life up on that mountain, she'd never seen the world and never even seen another giant. And so it was Orgulla didn't know she was a giant only in her mind, or that the god she thought she saw was just a boy, a boy named Jack.

Orgulla watched the god come closer, looming high, so high that he was like a mountain. "Welcome!" cried Orgulla in a regal voice, and when the god seemed not to hear, she hollered, "Yoo-hoo, god! I'm here!" But still the god did not look down, and as the cow trudged on, Orgulla feared she'd missed her chance. She took a running leap. She grabbed hold of the cow's tail. She hoisted herself up on its back. She waved and shouted, "Hey, god! Down here! It's me, Orgulla the Great!"

Jack didn't hear the tiny voice. He was too busy gazing at the mountains spread beneath him. How high up he was! No one anywhere in all the world was higher! Yes! He'd done it! Climbed the highest mountain!

Jack stood up. He cupped his hands around his mouth and shouted, "I am Jack, Conqueror of Mountains!" and when he heard the mountains echo back, "I am Jack, Conqueror of Mountains . . . Mountains . . . Mountains!" Jack shouted out again, for he felt mighty proud.

Orgulla got annoyed. "What are you, blind?" she cried, and stomped her foot down on the cow, which got so spooked it bolted, throwing god and giant from her back.

"Ouch!"

Jack landed on his rear; Orgulla landed on Jack's nose. She jumped, excited as a flea. She yelled, "Hey, god! Look here! Look at me!" But still this silly god refused to see, and so Orgulla bit him.

"Ouch!" cried Jack again, and when he saw a bug was on his nose, he flicked it off and sent Orgulla soaring through the sky.

Oh, happy day! Oh, happy, happy day! This was the moment that Orgulla had been waiting for! The god had sent her up to heaven! Soon she'd be a star! The giant spread her arms out wide, prepared to be immortal.

Meanwhile, down below, Jack was scrambling, falling over rocks and getting bruised and scraped.

"Ootch! Ouch!"

The cow had left him back behind. Already she was halfway down the mountain. "Stop! Wait up!" he cried. "Wait up for me!" But she kept going, didn't pay him any mind.

Conqueror of Mountains—hah!

Jack stumbled after, didn't notice when a tiny giant in the sky began to fall and called out, "Helllllp!" a cry that lasted down down down till she landed in a snowbank far below.

Plip!

THE GREEN QUEEN

Everywhere there was only fog and no birds sang.

Clop, clop, clop, clop.

On one side of the path the ground dropped off, but how far down was lost in fog. Jack tossed a pebble in but never heard it land. It seemed like there was nothing down there but the fog—no sea, no ground—and Jack supposed this was the very end of Earth.

Clop, clop, clop, clop.

The fog was thick, so thick Jack couldn't tell his left from right, his after from before.

Clop, clop, clop, clop.

Feeling cold and lost and all alone, Jack trembled, wished that he was anywhere but here. He told himself life wasn't fair, not fair at all. He envied boys who had a home and had a mama who would hold them tight when they got scared.

"Mama! Where's my mama? Mama!"

Clop, clop, clop, clop.

The cow came to a stop before a giant castle looming like a cliff from out the fog. It was a black and gloomy place and made Jack scared. To chase away his fear, he whistled, which he shouldn't ought have done, for whistling was illegal there on penalty of death by order of the Green Queen, the giant of that castle.

This Green Queen was a nasty sort, the vilest of the vile. She'd never known a happy moment in her life, at least not since the days when she was still the Princess Giant and her parents, then the King and Queen, had found a human baby on their doorstep.

"Poor dear!" the monarchs cried. They took the infant in, adopted her, and said she'd be their youngest princess. From the first, the baby was a gentle, cheerful thing. She smiled and smiled so much she got the castle smiling, too, so she was called the Happy Princess, and they all adored her.

All of them but one.

The Princess Giant wanted to be loved the way her human sister was, or even more. To make herself seem happier, the giant smiled gigantic smiles that covered half her face. But nobody believed them. Then the Princess Giant turned to magic, started making potions, casting spells. This wasn't any better. Nothing that the giant did could make her happy like her sister, or as loved.

And so it was that envy, like a snake, crawled inside her giant heart and sent its poison through her veins and turned her skin a pale and sickly green and made her hate, loathe, and despise the Happy Princess.

It went on like this for years. The princesses grew up, and by and by the King and Queen got old and died, which meant the Princess Giant got to be the Queen.

Unhappy day!

The first thing that the new Queen did was kick the younger princess out and banish her into the wilderness. The Happy Princess tried to make the best of things. She found an old abandoned cottage, fixed it cozy nice

and planted out a garden, grew some food
and lots of flowers. She would have been
content if only she'd had someone she could
share it with, but by and by the loneliness got
to her and the Happy Princess became sad.

This pleased the Queen.

Then one day a funny little man knocked
on the cottage door, told the princess he was
hungry, asked her for some food. She said,
"Come in," and shared her meal. In return,
the funny little man gave her a bean, a bean
he said was magic, good for just a single wish.
One wish was all the princess needed,
though. She shut her eyes and made a wish,
and when she looked, a baby boy was in her
arms, and she was happier than ever.

This wasn't good.

The moment that the Queen heard what

had happened, she got so full of envy that her spit turned green. She couldn't stand it, vowed she would destroy her sister's happiness once and for all. She made a spell that changed the Happy Princess to a beast that never smiles or laughs.

Poof!

"Moo," said the Happy Princess.

The Green Queen cackled. "Happy now, you stupid cow?" Next she gave an order to her soldiers, told them, "Kill the child!" Except they couldn't do it, couldn't bring themselves to kill a baby boy, and so instead they sneaked him far away and left him on a miller's doorstep, hoping he'd be safe.

For a while, the Green Queen almost was a little happy. But before long she got to feeling envious of other things—the flowers, the birds, the sun. Because they all seemed happier than her, her royal heart began to twist, began to burn, and so she conjured up the fog that hid the flowers, silenced all the birds. To make things worse, she made a hateful law forbidding anyone to smile or laugh or sing or even whistle, and the penalty was death.

Jack, who whistled ignorant of any law, cried out in fright to see the castle gate fly open and the soldiers rush out to surround him, grab him up, and take him to the Queen.

She said, "How dare you whistle in my kingdom? By law no one is happier than me. Prepare to die."

Jack said, "I wasn't whistling from happiness."

The Queen could see that what Jack said

was true. The poor boy looked so fearful and cast down it touched the wicked giant's heart, since nothing made her happier than someone else's sorrow. "Sweet thing," she said, and patted both her thighs. "Sit on my lap and tell me all about it."

Jack did some thinking fast. From how things looked, his best bet was to make her pity him and so he told a corker, said how he and his beloved mama used to live together. He told how she'd worked hard, he'd gone to school, and never was there any family happier till then one awful night his mama, she got kidnapped. When Jack went off to find her, it was awful. He'd died nearly a hundred deaths from starving and from shipwreck and from illness, and he'd battled off a thousand enemies while searching everywhere all over, high and low, but still he couldn't find his mother. "And now I guess I'll never see my mama's face again!" said Jack, who played his part so well he even fooled himself and got to crying so he couldn't stop.

The Queen was happy with Jack's story, thought, "Poor child!" and was about to pardon him, but then she noticed her own soldiers weeping, sobbing out of pity for the boy, and straightaway her envy rushed in through an unexpected door.

How dare her soldiers cry over a runt, a whining, useless nothing of a boy! What was his puny suffering compared to hers, the sorrow of a Queen! Yet had her soldiers ever shed a tear for her? Never! No! Not one! She tossed Jack off her lap and said, "I won't

allow it! No one can be unhappier than me!"
She snapped her fingers, told the soldiers,
"Kill the boy and kill him now."

Except her soldiers didn't move. How
could they kill a poor defenseless boy who'd
suffered so?

"Weaklings!" sneered the Queen, and
grabbed a sword to do the deed herself. But
Jack was sly and told her, "Thank you, Queen!
Please, kill me quick! End my sad and tragic
life! Make me happy at last!"

Happy at last? That pulled the Queen up
short. If she killed the boy and he'd be happy
dead, then he'd be happier than her forever.
Oh, no! That couldn't be! She scowled, she
growled, she couldn't stand the thought! No,
no! The boy must live and live to suffer.

Yet if he lived, her soldiers all would pity

him, and that was more than she could bear! She groaned, she moaned, that mustn't come to pass! No, no! The boy must die!

But if he died and death would make him happy, happier than her—she pulled her hair to stop the thought! No, no! It couldn't be! The boy must live!

And so it went, the Queen's tormented mind all tempest tossed—Die! Live! Die! Live!—but there was no way out. No matter what she did, the only end was envy, envy, envy, and she started to go mad. Her eyes went wild, she turned a brighter shade of green, and then she felt an awful pain inside her chest as envy ate her heart out till there wasn't any left.

The wretched creature fell down dead.

THE END

No one moved and no one spoke.

Then something happened. Because the Queen was dead, her spells died, too, and out of all the quiet there came change. The fog was first to go and opened up to let the sun come shining through. That made the flowers bloom and got the birds to sing. Jack was so amazed how everything was different that he didn't see the change that also happened to his cow. The soldiers noticed, though, and fell down on their knees, overjoyed to see their Happy Princess with them once again.

"The Queen is dead! Long live the Queen!"

"Hail, Happy Princess!" cried the soldiers, and they crowded round her, talking all at once in such excitement that Jack couldn't figure out what happened.

"But if the Queen is dead," said Jack, "then who's the Queen? And where's my cow?"

A soldier said, "Your cow's the Happy Princess!"

"Not the princess," said another. "She's the Queen!"

"My cow's a queen?"

"The Queen is dead! Long live the Queen!"

Nothing that they said made sense. Jack asked, "So who's the Happy Princess?"

"That used to be my name," said the woman standing where his cow had been.

THE END

At her voice, the soldiers all fell silent. They made a path as she walked up to Jack and knelt before him, held his face in both her hands. Jack's mind felt much confusion, but the woman's eyes were warm and quiet, kind. She looked at Jack in such a way as no one ever had before, as if she knew him inside out, the good and the bad, and loved him all the same. And then she called him Jack, her darling Jack, her son, the brave, truehearted boy who'd fought the giants and had saved his mother, now the Queen.

Jack said, "Hold on a second. Let me get this straight. You're my mother?"

"Yes."

"But you used to be my cow?"

"Yes."

"And now you are the Queen?"

"And you're the Prince."

"Whoa," said Jack, and shook his head in disbelief that such a thing could happen. Still, he didn't want to argue with such happy news and gave way to a smile that got the others smiling, too. Then Jack became so happy that he couldn't help but cry. That got everybody else to crying, too, and when they all had blubbered till they couldn't blubber anymore, the Queen was crowned and said they had to have a party. So they did, and everybody sang and danced and had a feast. And it went on for days.

As her first act of office, the Queen gave everyone a piece of land so they could have a garden for their food and flowers. Next, she divvied up the royal gold and shared it round till there was nothing left, and in that way made sure that no one in her kingdom ever had too little or too much and everyone could have enough.

She only ever made three laws. The first law said that everybody should please smile at least three times a day, and if they wanted, they could also sing a song. The second law decreed that any children with no parent should please come to live with her and Jack inside the castle, they'd be family. And the third law ordered that every cow should please be treated better than the Queen, so in that kingdom from then on when anybody met a cow, they bowed down low.

As for Jack, at last he'd got himself a home where he was wanted, and his job as Prince was keeping all the kingdom safe. Every morning he'd head off and deal with troublemaking giants, have adventures, and he almost never got back home till after dark. It was a perfect kind of life. And even though Jack still could be a bad boy now and then, he figured he was getting maybe almost pretty close to being good, or anyway to good enough. The proof was when his mother tucked him into bed each night, she always kissed him on the head and told him how she loved him more than ever every day.